The Devil May Care

A *Customizable Multi-Narrative Book*

by MJ Carambat

Cover Art by Eric Hibbeler

The Devil May Care
A Customizable Multi-Narrative Book

Copyright © 2013 by MJ Carambat

ISBN: 978-0-9912468-3-0

Printed in the United States of America

December 2013

Everyone has a favorite book, cherished, careworn and kept close to their heart,

but did you ever wish that...

...Frank L Baum told us more about the Wicked Witch of the *North?*

...Jules Verne spent more time describing the engines of the Nautilus?

...Lewis Carroll offered an explanation of how the Red Queen rose to power?

Wouldn't it be great if a book tailored itself to your personal taste?

Well, this one does!

The story you are about to read is a customizable *Multi-Narrative*, experience. There is only **ONE** plot, with **ONE** beginning and **ONE** end, but there are **SEVEN** different ways to read this book.

YOU get to specify the way you want the story to be told. Don't worry. No matter how you choose, you won't miss any major plot elements. Your choice will serve only to *emphasize* the parts you are most interested in.

"The Devil May Care" is told from the vantage points of two worlds: Earth and Mars. Pick the one you'd like the story to elaborate on the most. Next, chose which *style* of story you'd prefer to read.

Here's how it works

Choose **one** icon that matches your set of preferences from the chart below:

 **From Earth** Told in a Character-Driven Style

 **From Mars** Told in a Character-Driven Style

 **From Earth** Told in a Technology-Driven Style

 **From Mars** Told in a Technology-Driven Style

 **From Earth** Told in an Intrigue-Driven Style

 **From Mars** Told in an Intrigue-Driven Style

At the top of every section in the story you will see one or more of these icons. If your icon is **NOT** among them, you should skip over that section, moving down until you find YOUR icon.

This will insure you only read only the parts of the book you are most interested in.

If you'd prefer to read every single word in the book, *you can do that too!* This is the seventh way to read this book. The narrative is written so you can completely ignore the self-abridging options. You may start at the beginning and work your way all the way to the bottom, just like a regular novel.

Ready? Lets get started >>

Table of Contents

Nightmares

Earth | South America, Guiana Space Centre

Trevor Cadogan couldn't sleep. The demon was back, filling his head. Wicked-sharp claws, stubby curving horns and a viscous forked tale, long and scaly. The thing stood there, shifting back and forth, mocking him, silhouetted against an angry, red glow. The smoky half-light invoked a debilitating terror, flooding his mind with a premonition of doom fanned by the flames of hell.

The Welsh engineer sat bolt upright in bed, eyes wide with terror. "Get out of my head you infernal beastie!" His chest heaved and beads of sweat stood out on his forehead. His eyes darted around the darkened room in a panic.

He pressed his hands to his head, and the hellish image faded, replaced by the concerned face of his wife. She slipped her arm around his shoulders. "The nightmare again?"

"Martha, I don't know what I'm going to do." He was close to sobbing. "It's every god-forsaken night. I don't think I can take much more of this, I really don't. I haven't gotten a decent night's sleep in weeks."

"It's the stress," she said in a soothing voice. "You're so close. You're nervous about the launch, that's all."

"Maybe. I don't know. It's getting worse. It's been so *real* lately."

She nestled closer to him, and rubbed his tense shoulders, "Don't worry, love. It'll be better in the morning. Try to get some sleep."

The recurring hellish image plagued him night and day whenever he thought about the space probe—*his probe*—the one that would be launching day after tomorrow. Although Cadogan was confident the rocket and its complex payload would be ready in time, the demon persisted in taunting him.

"What's it all mean?" he groaned to himself, trying not to disturb his wife. He reviewed the equipment checklist in his mind, trying to dispel the grinning apparition.

He thought about the flight telemetry electronics, the power and backup systems, the thrusters, the robotics and camera equipment, and finally the launch rocket itself.

It was ready. Yet, the demon acted as if it knew otherwise. As if no matter how hard he worked, the project was going to fail—*he* would fail—and it was mocking him. Laughing maniacally at how the world's first privately funded space probe would never get off the ground.

He tried to ignore the sharp teeth, the scrape of its claws, but as the launch window loomed closer, the crimson devil grew more and more vivid. He wasn't sure he could maintain his sanity.

A privately built space probe was an expensive endeavor and Cadogan couldn't afford to make mistakes—*mistakes* weren't in the budget. Little else was either. On such a shoestring, it was a miracle he was able to build it at all, much less send it to another planet.

Unexpectedly, the project had met with much resistance. Even though Cadogan Aerospace provided rockets for governments around the world, none of them took his proposal seriously. Even NASA was unsupportive, unwillingly to supply any information or research not already in the public domain. No one believed the private sector could accomplish such a complicated endeavor on its own.

Well, there's a first time for everything, he thought. Demons or not, this bird was going to fly.

Interview

Mars | Outskirts of Taal City

Daz gunned his dune scooter hard. It roared over the sand, its huge, soft wheels distorting wildly with the increase in speed. The canyon below beckoned to him, but he had an appointment. He looked at his *chrono*, then at the canyon, then at the fuel gauge. *It would be close, but Eratz would wait for him wouldn't he?* He smiled, and banked his scooter into the gully.

After a thorough exploration of the area, Daz settled on a cool place out of the sun to look for fossils. He had an extensive collection at home. The hobby took the water riots off his mind. *Too many people in Taal City and never enough to drink. He wished someone would do something about the problem.*

"Daz, where are you?" piped his friend's voice from inside his pack.

He looked up at the sky in dread. The sun had risen significantly since he had climbed down here. He fished out the comm. "Um…Hi Eratz. What's got your nubs?"

"Stop picking on my horns and tell me you're almost here."

Daz winced, remembering the *interview*. He answered, "I'm in the vicinity, *yes*."

"Look buddy, I'm putting my flipping tail on the line for you. You want this job or not?"

Daz thought about it, *Want the job?—No. Want food and fuel credits?—Yes.*

"Eratz, I'm sorry, but something's come up. Can I come by tomorrow?"

"*Crubz,* Daz. This is the last time. This job is important to the city. The tunnels we're digging will bring the water we need."

"I know, I know..." said Daz. Then, he added mentally, *as long as it brings credits too.*

"Tomorrow, then. No excuses," demanded Eratz.

"I'll be there. You have my word."

"Yeah, like that means much. Sometimes you act like such a youngling."

Daz was offended. "I'm a full *solar* older than you!"

"Buddy, you're a smart guy. Why don't you see what's right in front of you?"

Daz kicked over a boulder and watched the shadow bugs scatter. "What do you mean?"

"Since I've known you, you've had, let's see...what is it? Over *fifteen* jobs?"

"That's not so uncommon."

"Daz, we met just two *solars* ago! By the way, you're late on the rent again."

"Tomorrow, Eratz. I'll be there tomorrow. Don't worry about the rent."

He shouldered his pack and mounted his scooter. He wasn't in the mood for more fossil hunting. Why did everything have to be so difficult? It wasn't his fault there was a water shortage. It's not like he caused the ancient canals on the surface to dry up.

He kicked a rock, sending it arcing over the canyon floor. The stupid oceans disappeared into underground aquifers thousands of *solars* ago. Sure, the tunnels were important, he just wished he didn't have to be one of the ones that had to dig them.

The job Eratz proposed for him wasn't exactly stimulating, but the work wasn't too strenuous and the *Taal*

Desert was interesting place. He might even dig up a few fossils.

He gunned the engine and the scooter bounded out of the canyon. He'd have to remember this place. The new specimens would make handsome additions to his collection.

Daz opened the door to his apartment and flopped down on the couch. It was a relief to be out of the hot sun. Eratz would be annoyed with him when he got back from work. He'd surprise him by having dinner ready. He turned the kitchen comm to a news program and put a pan on the heater coil.

He wanted to hear more on the story he'd been following over the last few days. Another archeologist was missing. The two men were exploring one of the ancient abandoned cities, and their colleagues suspected foul play. *Planetary Security* was investigating the case.

Now that he thought about it, it seemed like many people were disappearing lately. A woman living on a livestock farm in the *Greater Desert* reported her husband missing a few days ago. He told her he was on his way back with something he found in the field, but he never arrived. The authorities found no trace of him.

Daz thought the disappearances were very unusual, but what could he do about it? He cut up some *Farvel* roots and put them in the pan. *That's why we've got Planetary Security.*

Sabotage

Earth | South America, Guiana Space Centre

Martha Cadogan woke to find her husband had already left their apartment for work. His recurring nightmares were depriving him of sleep and she was concerned for him. If Trevor had a successful launch tomorrow, maybe his nightmares would stop—they had to. He acted as if he was in control, but she knew they were driving him mad.

Being so far from home wasn't helping either. Neither of them travelled much, and spending a few weeks at the remote South American launch facility had made them both homesick for the bustling cities of South Wales.

She consoled herself that it would all be over soon. Surely, things would be better when they returned to Cardiff after the launch.

* * *

From the control room, Cadogan watched the launch crew raise the rocket into the gantry against the brilliant yellow-orange glow of a South American sunrise. Beads of sweat formed on his brow as he struggled to ignore the screaming demon in his head. He was keeping the hellish image from affecting his composure, but just barely.

The past four years felt like a blur. So many problems, so many hurdles, and so little help from anyone outside his own backwater aerospace company. It was as if an elite few retained a monopoly on space exploration, keeping the club exclusive. No outsiders allowed—especially private sector interlopers.

Well, come the devil himself, Cadogan Aeorospace was going to Mars. With the help of the press, he had seen to that.

Tomorrow morning, newspapers around the world would announce the launch of the Outlander-I Martian Lander, riding atop Cadogan Aerospace's highly successful Vector II launch platform. In just a few months it would be in orbit around Mars. The lander would then make its descent, snapping high-resolution images of the surface.

Unlike Russian and American landers, the Outlander-I could hop from place to place using its thrusters. The public chose the landing sites via the internet. This was one of the reasons for the project's popularity. The lander was being billed as "a probe for the people."

The project owed its success to the public's enthusiasm. He was in their debt and he owed it to them to get a handle on these infernal visions. The menacing image of a horned, fork-tailed devil was getting more and more vivid and its demeanor had changed. It no longer simply taunted—it had grown outright threatening.

A tinny version of Elton John's "Rocket Man" rang from his pants pocket. He pulled out his cell phone and checked the number on the screen. It oddly read all five's. He held it to his ear. "Hello? Trevor Cadogan here."

He heard shallow breathing—or was that *sobbing?* He inquired again, "Hello?"

"Trevor..." spoke a terrified voice. "It's Martha. Please...I'm so scared."

"Martha? What's wrong? What's happened?" His grip on the cell phone tightened.

"They've blindfolded me…I'm…" He heard a frightened whimper, then someone else took the line. The voice sounded course and artificial, electronically altered. "Trevor Cadogan, you will do exactly as I say or your wife dies. Do you understand?"

"No, I don't bloody well understand! Who is this? Where's my wife?"

"She's safe as long as you cooperate. Now listen carefully. I have a job for you."

The man on the phone was probably a lunatic, but he had kidnapped his wife. For now, he had no recourse but to follow his instructions. He looked up at the rocket gantry and counted three technicians up there, working on the probe capsule. He waited until they left, then took the elevator to the upper level.

His hands shook as he opened the capsule. He couldn't believe what he was about to do. *Why now? We were so close to launch...so close!* With some difficulty, he unscrewed the lander's protective housing, took a deep breath and removed it. He was committed now. The probe was irrevocably open to airborne contaminants. Not that it mattered. He was about to take a wrench to the works inside. With a heavy heart, he smashed the primary camera's optics, took a photo of the damage with his cell phone, then carefully resealed the housing.

Cadogan returned to his office in a daze and slumped into his chair, waiting for his phone to ring. He couldn't believe what he had just been forced to do to the Outlander-I's camera. He stared at the wrench on his desk in horror. Four years of hard, intensive work all wasted. He thought he'd never forget that sound. The sickening crack of the glass as his wrench shattered it into a hundred pieces. He closed his eyes and slowly shook his head.

"Rocket Man" broke the silence and sent a chill up his spine.

He held the phone to his ear. "It's done you bastard."

"I can see that. The picture you sent from your phone is quite clear. Good work, Cadogan."

"To hell with you. Where's Martha?"

The coarse, droning voice ignored him. "Incidentally, don't bother tracing the address you sent it to. It's a drop box and the account has already been deleted."

"Look, what's all this about, then? Who are you working for? Why are you doing this?"

"Mr. Cadogan, you wouldn't believe me if I told you. Let's just say the world isn't ready for your little interplanetary webcam just yet."

"Where's my wife?"

"As promised, you will find your wife safe at home. I urge you not try anything foolish before tomorrow's launch. We can always find you *and your wife* again."

Launch

Earth | *South America, Guiana Space Centre*

The next morning, the Vector II rumbled into the sky. It was a perfect launch, but Trevor Cadogan wasn't celebrating. The control room exploded into congratulations, but he had to turn his back to hide his rage and grief. They didn't know about the camera. No one would, until three months later when the space probe arrived at Mars.

Martha eased him aside and whispered, "It's not your fault, you know."

He looked at her incredulously. "I suppose the wrench shattered the camera's optics all by itself, did it? How is it *not* my fault? I was a coward to give in to his demands."

"I don't think you're a coward, husband. You were protecting *me*. You had no choice. You still don't. Neither of us does. We haven't seen the end of this."

"The man on the phone said we'd be left alone as long as I cooperated. I disabled the Outlander-I's camera, and he released you. So far, he's kept up his side of the bargain. As long as we don't go to the authorities, we should be okay."

"And you believe this coming from the bunch of thugs that kidnapped and threatened to kill me?"

"They were hardly thugs, dearest. They're too well informed and organized. They knew exactly when the capsule was being sealed. If I had gone up there an hour earlier, the damage would have been discovered. Any later and I would have missed the window of opportunity."

"All your hard work, and everything we've sacrificed. It's just not fair."

Cadogan sighed. "No it's not. But at least the horned devil is gone."

Martha smiled, "You see, I told you it was stress. Now that the worst has happened, your demon can't complain."

"Nothing to complain about? How about that I'm wasting a three-hundred, million dollar rocket, to deliver a two-hundred, million dollar *blind* space probe to Mars?"

"I know, and I'm sorry. But what else could have made you see devils?"

"Martha, it got worse yesterday, right before the call. It was threatening me."

"It was *speaking* to you?"

"Towards the end, yes, it did. It didn't like the probe at all. It bloody well hated it. It cheered me on when I wrecked it, cackling and laughing with that horrible nasal of his. It was enjoying itself immensely."

"That's horrible."

"You have no idea. But by the time I got back to the office, it sort of just winked out. Haven't seen it since."

Well, Trevor Cadogan, you've got real demons to contend with now. I don't think this is the last we've seen of those people."

"I'm afraid you're right. Especially since I didn't completely disable the lander's camera."

Martha looked at him, eyebrows raised. "But I thought they told you to—"

"The man said he wanted me to blind the probe by shattering the lens. He didn't say to disable the electronics. An electronics malfunction would show up on the automated system's check before launch. What he didn't know was that the primary optics are protected by a plate glass cover. That's what I shattered—not the lens itself."

"But the photo—"

"Was of shattered glass inside the lens housing. Keep in mind, it'll be a small miracle if we can shake the debris free once the lander's in the atmosphere. And even so, without the protective cover, I don't know how long the camera will survive in Mars' hostile climate."

Martha crossed her arms and leveled her eyes at him. "Trevor, you're gambling with our lives."

"You said it yourself. They aren't going to leave us alone. I don't plan on just waiting around for the next three months. I'm going to find out who these people are and I'm going to stop them."

Free of the demon's distraction, Cadogan was thinking clearly for the first time in a long time.

"I think I know what they're up to, but I don't know why. I think they want to show the world what a waste of money it is to invest in private space exploration. Rockets blow up on the launch pad all the time, but the public will see a cracked lens as incompetent in the extreme. They mean to discredit us."

"If they didn't want your space probe to succeed, why did they let you build it in the first place?"

"I think we surprised them. I don't think they expected us to get this far, so fast and so publically. Think of all the resistance we met when we started. If it weren't for the popular sentiment, we never would have gotten off the ground. It feels like there's some sort of global agenda to keep us out of deep space."

"I never thought my hyper-rational, super-skeptical husband would become a conspiracy theorist."

"I'm not. I'm a realist, and I'm going to fix this.

Reprimand

Mars | Taal Lesser Desert Excavation & Tunnel Works

Daz pulled open the big iron door and let himself inside the quarry complex. The door slammed shut behind him and nearly clipped his tail. After his interview three months ago, he was now *Workman* Daz. The moniker still made him cringe. He quickened his pace down the hallway. He was late—*again. Why did they have to start so early anyway?*

He hefted a large, wheel-shaped object out of his pack. Its discovery on the way over had made him late. Well, late-*er*. Surely, someone in the geolab upstairs could tell him what it was.

He looked at time clock. *Oh crubz, the foreman's gonna blow a gasket this time.* The geo lab visit would have to wait. He put the artifact in his locker and changed into his coveralls, folding his small, vestigial wings inside.

Everyone else had already donned their protective gear and moved out. He hurried to the lift, adjusting his hard hat to better accommodate his horns, pulled the gate shut and rode down into the quarry.

Daz found the rest of the miners huddled against a large boulder, straining to hear a briefing from the foreman in the howling wind. He found a place next to his friend Eratz, and tried to look inconspicuous. It didn't work.

"If it isn't workman Daz!" shouted the foreman in mock surprise. "So nice of you to join us this morning. Did you get enough sleep this time? I hope so, because I've got a *special* job for you."

"If it's all the same sir, I have an excuse this time. I found something. It's back in my locker."

"Workman, I don't care if you found the Lost Sceptre of Taal. You're now on extended shift duty in the Whistler, to make up for your lost time. Get down there and start drilling. I don't want to see you again for twelve cycles."

Eratz shrugged his shoulders, giving him a *well, what did you expect?* expression.

Daz sulked. Piloting the Whistler was noisy, hot and tedious, but that wasn't what bothered him. With the extended shift, he wouldn't have a chance to visit the lab.

"Eratz, do me a favor, would you? Can you run something I found by Doctor Havarti? It's in my locker."

"What is it?"

"I don't know. It's something found it in the desert on my way in this morning. I thought maybe the doc would know."

"If I have the time. I'll let you know what he says when you get out of the hole." Then his tone softened a little, "Good luck."

Daz thanked his friend and headed to the equipment bay where the Whistler waited for him.

The foreman had every right to be angry, but this was too much. After all, he was only a half-cycle late this time. He'd probably be looking for another job soon, especially if he kept getting shifts in the Whistler as punishment. He didn't think his ears could take much more. He inserted his earplugs and started the machine, wincing at the high-pitched whine.

The large sonic drilling machine employed high frequency sound waves to pummel the rock into rust-colored dust. Besides the stomach-churning vibrations of the drill, the pilot's cab offered little in the way of comfort. It was hot, cramped and smelled of sweat.

He punched twelve cycles into the automatic timer and the machine lurched forward. Soon, he'd be ensconced in rock with clouds of red dust billowing out behind him. The lumbering behemoth wouldn't stop and back out until his shift was over. It inched forward, slow as a rock-eating gully leech. He flipped on the monitors and began the mind-numbing watch for dangerous changes in the strata.

His thoughts drifted to the strange artifact he had found. It had glinted in the sun as he rambled his dune scooter around the ridge of Asper Crater. He detoured to investigate and found the peculiar metallic object sticking halfway out of the sand in the middle of nowhere.

He dug it out, surprised at how light it was and shoved it in his pack. Rumors of odd artifacts out here were just rumors, weren't they? Had he actually found one? His excitement evaporated when he discovered his scooter wouldn't start. Dust clogged the intake. He did his best to clear it, but after several false starts, he resigned himself to dragging it the rest of the way to work.

Daz looked at the Whistler control panel, only eight cycles so far. Never one to break a promise, his friend would have brought the artifact to Dr. Havarti for him by now. In another four cycles his shift would be over and he'd catch up with his friend. With his abused ears, he wondered if he'd even be able to hear what Eratz had to say.

The Whistler screamed into the rock. *Gods,* how he hated the sound the tunneling machine made as it vibrated the rock to dust. Okay, he'd been late three days in a row, but did that justify a twelve cycle on this beast? It didn't seem fair.

Daz took a drink from his meager water allowance, shaking the last drop out of the canteen. In another five solars the vast network of tunnels would be complete, and the planet's water supply problems would be over.

The water was just one issue the council had to deal with. Strange sightings were increasing all over the planet and people were getting nervous. By now, everyone, including him, had seen the dim lights cruising lazily across the sky, but no one knew what they were. There were lots of reports on the news comm. *Hadn't a few of them come crashing down? Why didn't anyone ever find anything?*

His thoughts turned to the wheel he found near the crater. *Could it be related?* He wondered what Dr. Havarti would think. He owed Eratz another dinner. Not for just bringing Havarti the wheel, but for making him look bad by being late all the time.

The Whistler disengaged and reversed up the tunnel, catching him by surprise. He still had four cycles left in his shift. He pressed the comm button.

"Foreman? What's going on? I'm not done yet."

He waited for an answer, and called again. No response. Only static filled his headset.

Captured

__Mars__ | Taal Lesser Desert Excavation & Tunnel Works

Daz climbed out of the Whistler, dusted off his coveralls and removed his earplugs. His head rang from eight cycles of sonic drilling in the tunneling machine. Why had they called him out early? His tail twitched nervously. Something wasn't right. Removing his hard hat, he put a hand to his forehead to shield his eyes and scanned the ruddy terrain. The quarry was empty of personnel.

From out of nowhere, shock troops surrounded him, weapons drawn.

"Workman Daz, you are to accompany us immediately." One of the officers stepped forward and took him roughly by the arm. He couldn't help but notice the impressive size of the officer's horns. This was no seargent, this was a troop commander.

"What's going on? I don't understand. If this is about being late...I...I..."

The stern commander said nothing as he escorted Daz to a military transport and shoved him inside.

"Where are you taking me?"

The commander slammed the transport's door in his face, locking him inside the vehicle's dark interior. As his eyes adjusted in the dim light, he noticed two others already inside. He thought he recognized the one in the lab coat. *Was that Dr. Havarti?* Another captive in coveralls sat across from him on the bench, his face in shadow. He leaned forward to get a better look.

"Eratz!"

"Hi Daz. Nice day, eh?" His friend's lower lip dripped with blood.

"You look like you've been in a sand cow stampede," said Daz.

"I'm sorry buddy, I tried to protect you, I really did. But they were, well...*insistent.*" Eratz wiped his mouth with his sleeve.

"Protect me from what?"

"I tried to tell them *I* found the wheel, but they didn't believe me. I'd already told Dr. Havarti I was doing *you* a favor."

"I don't understand. Who are *they*? Why are they doing this?"

"Don't know. They showed up right after the doc made a call about your wheel. He was surprised as I was, when..."

Daz noticed his friend's sudden downcast expression, "What happened?"

"They got him too. That's him over there." He nodded to the crumpled heap near the end of the bench. "They beat him up pretty bad."

"*Oh gods*. I'm sorry I got you into this, Eratz. Do you still have the wheel?"

"They took it from Dr. Havarti. He didn't give it up easily, which is why they're bringing him too. It's probably up front, in the driver's cab with the commander."

"*Crubz*. Did Havarti have time to look at it? Did he tell you what it was?"

"Yeah, he looked at it but didn't know. Said he's never seen anything like it. He found some weird markings around its edge, in some unknown language. He wanted to get someone in cryptology to take a look at it, so he made a call over the comm."

Daz nodded. "So that's how the military found out about it. Did he tell you anything else?"

"He seemed to think it was part of something else. It looks damaged, like it broke off something bigger. But he's got no idea who made it."

"Why not?"

"Even after lots of testing, he's got no idea what it's made of."

The transport took its three captives deep into the desert, its eight wheels digging deep trenches in the shifting sand. The Commander yelled over the roar of the engine into the comm, his voice clearly audible through the cab's rusty metal wall.

"Yes sir, i've got them. The two boys and the doctor." There came a pause. "No sir, not at first. Havarti was very reluctant. He required some *persuasion.*" Another pause. "Yeah, we got em soon enough. One hundred percent containment."

Daz whispered to his friend, "What's he talking about?"

Eratz shrugged, then motioned for him to be quiet. The Commander was speaking again.

"Are you sure you don't want me to run the interrogation?" A pause. "No sir, I'm not questioning your authority. It's just at your age..."

The Commander must have pulled the comm out of his ear, because just for a moment, Daz could hear a high-pitched, nasal voice screaming obscenities at the man.

"I apologize, sir. I was simply concerned for your health." Another long pause. "Yes sir. I'm approaching the complex now. Transport 633 out."

After the conversation terminated, they heard the Commander utter one last clear statement associating the diminutive size and shriveled shape of the old man's horns to that of his reproductive organ.

Orbit

Earth | *Cardiff, Wales*
Cadogan Aerospace Mission Control Center

On a large wall monitor in the Outlander-I Mission Control Center, the computer superimposed a blue ellipse surrounding a simulated view of Mars. A tiny red dot marked the space probe's current position. It had settled into a perfect aero braking orbit. Another milestone. Another brief round of applause. Cadogan tried to share his staff's enthusiasm.

In a few days, the "People's Probe" would be in position to drop into the Martian atmosphere and then the real fun would begin. He didn't relish the prospect. His celebrity status would take a nose-dive the moment the camera went active.

His phone rang. The display showed all fives, and his stomach turned inside out.

"Hello, Cadogan."

He recognized the digital voice immediately.

"Congratulations, on a successful orbit."

"What? You again? I thought we were quits." He wondered how he knew about the orbit. They'd released nothing.

"We were. You, apparently, were not. You've been making inquiries. *Naughty, naughty.*"

His blood ran cold. So that's why he hadn't heard from the private investigator. After a long string of dead ends, Cadogan had found the specialist through a series of obtuse contacts. The man charged him an exorbitant fee, and then vanished. He assumed the man simply ran off.

His eyes darted around the room in a panic. *Where was Martha?*

"Look Cadogan, I'm going to make this simple for you. Back off. You're prying into things you don't understand. Last warning."

He couldn't find his wife among the technicians. "Where's my wife? What have you—"

"Relax Cadogan, she went to use the ladies. Oh look, she's come back."

The caller hung up and the door of the control room opened. Martha stepped inside.

"Hi dearest. Did I miss anything?"

Cadogan crossed the room, took her in his arms and hugged his surprised wife.

"Oh my," she said. "What are we celebrating?"

Ashen-faced, he whispered, "They know about the private investigator."

"What? How could they possibly?"

"They're watching us. They've had us under surveillance all this time. I'm surprised they don't know about the lens cover."

"I think you're being a little paranoid."

"Martha, when I asked where you were, he told me you were in the loo."

She stared at him, eyes wide. He watched her surprise harden into anger.

"We're running out of time," said Cadogan. "In a few days, my guys will be working on the camera, getting it functional again. They'll know that the damage extends only to the lens cover. If they fix it before we find out who is behind this…"

The control room technicians cheered as the probe successfully completed a complex deceleration burn.

Cadogan sighed. *They were one step closer to landing on Mars.*

Cadogan knew that look. Martha was furious about having her privacy invaded. He watched her bristle with anger, but hold her tongue in the crowded room.

"Excuse me, captain, but I have the latest orbital figures." Codagan's chief science officer wore a lewd red pin on his lab coat with the phrase, *Engineers Do It Without The Manual.*

Cadogan smiled and took the thin tablet. Orbital telemetry. It all looked depressingly accurate. Why couldn't something just go wrong all on its own?

"Thanks, Roberts. Looks good to me. Can you check the fuel consumption rate on the number six thruster?"

The chief science officer returned to his console and Martha drifted back to her husband's side.

"Trevor, I don't care if they know the size of my knickers—I'm a size eight, by the way, thank you very much—but this stops now. How do they know so much?"

Cadogan's eyes searched the room, seeking the corners, the fixtures. "Hidden cameras, maybe? Probably just tracking devices. I'll need to sweep the entire complex for bugs and review all staff clearances.

Martha was impervious to bad news. It was one of the many things Cadogan loved about her. Rather than being fearful of the caller's threats, she was mad as a hornet.

"If only that private investigator had turned up something. We certainly paid him enough."

Cadogan tapped his chin. "It's strange. We haven't heard from him in months, but he must be working on the case, otherwise why did I get that call?"

"That means these people aren't impossible to find," said Martha. "He must be on to something."

"Either than, or he's dead."

Interrogation

Mars | *An Undisclosed Location near Taal City*

Daz stopped screaming for help nearly two cycles ago. He sat tied to a chair in the middle of a large, darkened room in a circle of dim light. The rope dug painfully into his arms and legs and he was very thirsty.

If they were trying to intimidate him, they were doing a great job. He wondered how Eratz and Dr. Havarti were doing back in their confinement cell. *Were they being interrogated as well?*

"Can I get a drink of water at least?" His voice echoed in the large room. "You've got the wrong citizen! I haven't done anything wrong."

"Water is an expensive commodity," intoned a high-pitched voice directly in front of him. Daz looked up to see a wrinkled hand emerge out of the gloom. It held a glass of water. "But I see no reason for *unnecessary* cruelty."

Daz felt someone behind him cut the ropes binding his arms. Daz rubbed some life back into them, took the glass and drained it. The man sitting in front of him grinned. He seemed to have too many teeth.

"You may call me Special Inquisitor Kul."

Daz nodded, confused. *What was Planetary Security doing in Taal city?*

The Inquisitor held something to the light. "Tell me workman, where did you find this?"

Daz squinted at the wheel the wizened old man held in his long, bony fingers. "In the desert. On my way to…"

Kul slapped him hard, sending the glass flying. He heard it shatter over the ringing in his ears.

"What part of the desert? My time is valuable, boy. Don't waste it."

"No sir...sorry sir. Near Asper Crater, along the western ridge. It was sticking out of the stand." For a moment, the Inquisitor's intense stare focused its attention over Daz's shoulder, catching the eye of the officer standing behind him. The Commander saluted and walked briskly out of the room.

"Who else have you told about this?"

Frightened as he was, Daz considered his options. His friends' lives were probably at stake. Somehow, he needed to buy more time. He decided to send himself into *catalepsy*. Over millions of years of evolution, the ancient fear response was no longer automatic in his people, but it could be induced. It would be easy considering how fast his hearts were beating. His eyes rolled back and he blacked out.

"Daz? Wake up! Can you hear me?" Eratz's voice sounded distant, miles away.

"C'mon son. Wake up. They're going to be back soon." Dr. Havarti tried to raise him into a standing position, but both of them collapsed against the wall. The doctor wasn't in much better shape. He scowled at Eratz. "A little help here would be nice."

Eratz helped them up. He slapped at Daz's cheeks until his eyes opened. "You freaking lunatic, you could have died pulling that stunt."

Daz rubbed his aching head. "C'mon, it's not so dangerous. We did it as kids, remember? It used the scare the *crubz* out of our parents."

Eratz chuckled at the memory. "What I meant is that you're lucky *they* didn't kill you. What did they want from you anyhow?"

"It was the Special Inquisitor. He wanted to know where I found the wheel, and who I told about it. That's why I went cataleptic. I thought it'd buy us some time."

The doctor nodded. "That wheel is alien technology. Why else would Planetary Security be involved? I have no doubt they mean to kill us once they're satisfied no one else knows about it."

Daz looked at his frightened friend and smiled. "Well then, let's get out of here."

The cell was small, windowless and had one door. Luckily, Daz was imprisoned with his two friends, which made things much easier. Since waking up, and to the amazement of himself and his friend, he had formed an escape plan. *Since when did he start taking the initiative?*

Daz pulled a multi-tool out of his inner pocket, surprised the guards had missed it, and tossed it to Dr. Havarti. The doctor unscrewed the light switch's metal wall plate, and pulled the wires out carefully. The lights went out, replaced by the dim red glow of emergency lighting.

"We're in luck," said Havarti. "This room is fed by two independent circuits. I can run them in series and double our voltage."

Daz nodded. "Good, but be careful you don't electrocute *yourself* when you reattach the wall plate."

You're sure there was only one guard in the corridor?"

"That's all that was out there when they brought you in, but I don't know if there are any security cameras in the hall," said Eratz.

"We'll just have to risk it." Daz dropped to the floor, and pretended to convulse.

Eratz banged on the door. "My friend is sick. He's shaking all over. Please, open up!"

Within a few seconds, they heard keys jingling.

"Stand away from the door or be shot," said the guard.

The door swung wide and he stepped inside, weapon drawn. "Step away from the prisoner, both of you. Hands where I can see them."

Daz kicked spasmodically as his friends backed against the wall.

"Why are the lights off in here?" asked the guard suspiciously. He reached for the light switch and his eyes went wide as a surge of electricity pulsed through his body. The guard emitted a stifled yelp and went rigid. He collapsed to the floor, his photon rifle rolling to Daz's feet.

"Well, that was easy," said Daz, picking up the weapon. They raced to the transport bay.

"I don't know which god you pray to, but I want his comm number," said Eratz.

Havarti grinned. "Me too."

Daz didn't know if it was a delayed side effect of waking from catalepsy, but he felt a sense of euphoria. The trick of shocking the guard with their confinement cell's lighting panel had been his idea, and to his astonishment, it had worked. Havarti and Eratz were looking to *him* for their next move. *How had that happened?*

The transport had been difficult for the doctor to hotwire. Daz glanced at the damaged instrument console. "I can't tell how much fuel we have." The machine rumbled out of the hanger and they set off across the desert, throttle wide-open.

Havarti sighed. "I've long suspected the Planetary Security Council was hiding evidence of extraterrestrial life. Too many of my colleagues have gone missing."

"I think most people believe that," said Eratz. "It's just no one has any proof."

"We did, until they took it." Daz veered the transport sharply to avoid a boulder. The dust made for poor visibility. "I still can't believe it was from another planet."

"They were certainly interested in it," said Havarti. "You probably don't remember, but when I was your age, there was a controversial discovery near the northern pole."

"You mean the Altrusian Meteorite?" asked Daz.

"Yes, but a lot of folks think the Altrusian government created the meteorite story to cover what actually impacted up there. Within months of the discovery, every expedition member died."

"Yes, but that was because of complications due to exposure."

"If that's what you want to believe."

Landing Sequence

Earth | *Cardiff, Wales*
Cadogan Aerospace Mission Control Center

Cadogan paced the control room like an expectant father. They had made no progress tracing the call, nor did he find any hidden cameras or transmitters in the control room. He took another concerned look at the view screen.

In fifty-four minutes, the lander would execute its de-orbit burn and hurtle planet-ward over a vast, empty region known as the Meridiani Planum. Of all the landing locations voted on, *Endeavour Crater* was one of the most popular, and it was first on the Outlander-I's agenda. Everyone wanted to see the last resting place of NASA's defunct Opportunity rover. Martha joined his side at the control center's rear wall.

"I'm sorry I've put us in so much danger," he said. "Maybe it would be best if we scrub the mission. I could upload a virus to corrupt the landing sequence. That might satisfy them."

Martha looked horrified. "Trevor, this mission is more important than both of us. Don't you dare screw it up."

He admired his wife's courage, but how could he continue to put her in jeopardy? Still, her dedication to the project warmed his heart. His face flushed and his eyes glistened with tears.

"Martha, I can't lose you. I should have destroyed that lens."

"Dearest, I'm scared too, but you were right to do what you did. Think of it. Our greatest achievement as a species—to reach for the stars. And you're putting it within reach of the common man."

"But..."

"I'm a big girl Trevor, I know what I'm signed up for. We'll get through this. But promise me one thing."

"What is it?"

"That you'll do everything in your power to recover that space probe and make this mission a success. If you don't, then you've already lost me."

They were both weeping now, and making a scene. Cadogan wiped his eyes. "I swear, I'll keep you safe. As long as I live."

"I know you will, husband," whispered Martha, breaking their embrace. "Now, go land on Mars."

He turned to the view screen. Twenty minutes to Endeavor Crater. He squeezed Martha's hand and made his decision.

"Roberts, how does the telemetry look?"

"So far so good, Captain. Looking for anything in particular?"

The American had been calling him "captain" ever since Cadogan put him on staff. The technician had a fanatical love of Star Trek, and a twisted sense of humor. Exuberant personality aside, he was a brilliant research scientist, and quickly climbed the ranks to chief science officer, a title that made him laugh every time he heard it.

"How are we on fuel reserves? I want to come down hotter than normal."

"I wouldn't recommend it. There's some pretty turbulent winds in the lower atmosphere. She's gonna shake, rattle and roll."

"Good, that's what I want. I'd like to try and shake off some *debris* we might have accumulated."

"Aye sir," said Roberts uneasily. "You're cutting it close. We're just barely going to have enough time to send and confirm the new instructions before the descent."

"That's fine. Make it so," said Cadogan, doing his best Picard impression.

Four-hundred thousand feet above the surface of Mars, the Outlander-I received its instructions and divided into two separate components. The lander unit slowly drifted away from the orbital platform, which it would use as a communications relay.

Cadogan watched the lander's distance-delayed telemetry track a virtual course on the view screen. From here the Outlander-I was on its own. He hoped the last set of instructions he sent would do what they were supposed to. Roberts better have gotten it right; there was no way to make last minute adjustments.

The minutes ticked by. Cadogan watched the telemetry streaming back from the craft. His heart thumped louder and louder as the numbers became more erratic.

"Turbulence," said the chief science officer. "The increased rate of descent you ordered has her shaking, but it's nothing she can't handle. We're still on the bead, Captain."

"Roberts, please stop calling me that. I'm not your *captain*." Cadogan immediately regretted snapping at the American, but his nerves were on edge.

"Um, okay. Aye, *sir*." said the American, injured.

"Sorry, Roberts. Just nervous I guess," said Cadogan. *Nerves, but no demons. Thank god for small wonders.*

"Eleven minutes to braking thrusters," the chief science officer reported.

Cadogan nodded. The camera compartment would open thirty seconds after the maneuvering thrusters fired.

The moment of truth. He looked at the mission clock and a shiver ran down his spine. It had already happened. Because of the lag, the camera was already imaging by now. The first image would be here in a little under ten minutes. His fate was now streaming through space at light speed, completely unstoppable. His palms were sweating. He didn't know which he wanted to see more, the *fatal* surface of Mars, or a *life-giving* spider-web of cracked glass.

Cadogan fidgeted, waiting for the first image to arrive. "Rocket Man" broke the uneasy silence. The old Elton John tune made everyone jump.

"What the hell do you want now?" Cadogan hissed into the receiver, not even bothering to check the caller ID. "Can't you just leave us alone?"

"Cadogan, you're in danger," said the frantic caller.

His eyes went wide. It was the voice of the missing private investigator.

"I can't tell you much over the phone...I'm being followed. I don't know how much longer I can evade them. You have no idea—you have no *earthly* idea how big this conspiracy is. I need to...oh no, I've been spotted." There was the sound of a pistol being cocked. "Good luck, Cadogan."

Martha clutched his arm. "Who it them? What did they say?"

Before he could answer, the control room erupted with a cacophony of voices. Cadogan whirled around and caught his breath. The Outlander-I's first image from the red planet was streaming to the view screen.

The Lesser Desert

***Mars** | Lesser Taal Desert*

Daz considered how much his luck had changed over the past cycle. Waking from catalepsy, he'd found himself in the confinement cell with his two friends, protected by just one guard. Then, his improvised escape plan to get out had worked, much to his surprise, and Havarti managed to hot-wire a military transport.

He jerked the steering wheel hard to avoid a small crater appearing unexpectedly out of the dusty, star lit landscape. Eratz howled in pain as the doctor banged into him.

"Daz," said Eratz nursing his tail. "I think you're going the wrong way. Isn't that ridge supposed to be behind us?"

Havarti peered through a small side-window of abraded glass. "Yes, I agree. Taal City is the other way around."

Daz stared single-mindedly at the scene ahead. "We're not going to Taal City. We're going to Asper Crater."

"Oh no. He's planning something again," said Eratz, surprised they weren't going to ditch the transport and lay low somewhere, until this all blew over. That would have been more like the friend he knew.

"The crater is where the Commander went when I told the Inquisitor where I found the wheel. We need to know what else they're looking for. Do we still have the guard's rifle?"

"Right here." Dr. Havarti inspected the weapon they took off the unconscious security guard they left back in the cell. He smiled, recalling the boy's ingenuity in short-circuiting the lighting switch plate to accomplish this. An indicator on the photon rifle blinked red, and his smile changed to a grimace. "This rifle is useless. The energy cell is spent. It must have shorted out when we electrocuted the guard."

Eratz looked around. "Um, we've got no weapons. Daz, you still want to do this?"

Daz felt his luck draining away. What kind of trouble was he heading into now? Maybe they should just get the hell out of there. He was just some boy from Taal City, after all. He wished he had never found that blasted wheel.

He glanced at his battered companions. Eratz' lip was bleeding again and Havarti was favoring his right leg. The Special Inquisitor had ordered all this. His anger returned, his cheek flaring where the foul old man had struck him.

"Look, there's not much point in running," said Daz. "The Inquisitor will find us, no matter where we go. They're hiding something. Something they don't mind kidnapping or maybe even killing over. I don't care that it's Planetary Security doing this. No one should be above the law, we need to expose them."

Havarti nodded. "I wholeheartedly agree, son. Besides, I've got a little score to settle with the Commander." He shifted his battered leg to a better position.

"You know me, Daz," said Eratz, tailing flicking behind him. "I'm always up for a scrap."

"The Inquisitor wants whatever else is in that crater," said Daz. "Doc, you still think it was just a piece of debris?"

"Most likely. The wheel looked as if it came detached from something. But I doubt whatever it was would have crashed there, much less caused the crater. Asper Crater is millions of years old. Also, anything that small would have burned up as it fell through the atmosphere. In all likelihood, it rolled there on its own."

"Rolled there? Like it was part of some sort of vehicle?" asked Eratz.

"Precisely," said the doctor.

Daz cursed. "I don't care how it got there, we're going to stop them from hiding more evidence. The planet needs to know what they are doing."

Eratz leaned over and surveyed the windswept desolation. "I guess this means we'll be late for work tomorrow, eh?"

Daz glanced sideways at him. "Eratz, you're a genius. You've just given me a brilliant idea."

His friend looked at him quizzically, but Daz merely grinned and turned the transport to a new heading.

The photon rifle was useless, but Daz had his mind on a far more powerful weapon.

"Where are we going now?" asked Eratz, confused.

"I think I know where we can get a new energy cell for that rifle."

"We're going to need more than one rifle. There's bound to be an entire troop at the crater by now," said Dr. Havarti. "It's a large area, and they'll need a lot of people to perform the search,"

"Don't worry. I'm not planning on using *just* the rifle."

Eratz cast him a suspicious glance. "What are you up to Daz?"

"It's a surprise. I hope you brought your earplugs"

The drive was proving to be a long one. The dust had settled, and above them, the stars blazed brightly in the thin atmosphere.

Eratz strained his head to look closer, and banged his horns on the glass. One star, dimmer than most, cruised slowly across the sky. He pointed it out to the others. "What are those things, doc? Anybody know?"

"They started showing up when I was your age." Havarti said. "We have a pretty good idea of their size and orbital characteristics, but we've no idea what they could be."

"Yeah, I've heard stories," said Daz. "Some of them have fallen to the surface. Meteors maybe?"

"Perhaps, no one's ever found one," said the doctor. "If they are meteors, they aren't like anything we've seen before. For example, they have no discernable tail." He paused to emphasize his next statement. "Some think they're alien."

"Those little lights are alien spacecraft?" asked Eratz.

Havarti laughed. "Not unless they are very *tiny* aliens. Our telescopes resolve them to nothing more than blurry points of light, but we've been able to estimate their size. They largest is less than a third the length of this transport—too small to be spacecraft."

"What do you think they are?" asked Daz.

"Until yesterday, I might have scoffed at the idea. But the composition of that wheel you found was unlike anything I have ever seen. I think both the artifact and the lights are related. Most likely, they are probes from another planet."

Detours

Mars | *Taal Lesser Dessert*

The transport rumbled to a stop at its altered destination. Daz knew the quarry would be closed, but the gate to the equipment bay only had a simple chain and lock. Once they got down there, the multi-tool in his top pocket would make short work of that.

Havarti looked out the window. "The quarry? Why are we back at the quarry?"

"I think I know," said Eratz, smiling. He patted Daz on the back, and the two boys lept from the cab.

Daz turned to Dr. Havarti after he forced open the gate's lock.

"The irrigation tunnels connect Taal City with the northern provinces, where the water table is higher and easier to reach. The tunnels aren't very deep below the surface, so we had to go around Asper Crater. One of these tunnels runs directly below the western ridge, which is where I found the wheel."

"But we'll never get the transport down there," said Havarti.

"We're not taking the transport. After I find an energy cell for that photon rifle, we're taking the Whistler."

* * *

The Commander had found what they were looking for at the crater. The old man back at the complex would be pleased for a change. He secured the large alien artifact in the back of the transport, and climbed into the cab. The things he saw in this job never ceased to surprise him. The artifact had six wheels, one of which was missing, connected beneath a flat, shiny platform. Several tubular shafts protruded from its surface, with various appendages extending from its surface.

The other two troop transports got in line behind him and they made to head back. He reported his success over the comm then checked for the convoy in his rear-view mirror. They had vanished, replaced by towering column of dust. The ground shook and his own transport skidded backwards, trying to regain traction. *What was happening?* He was falling. Falling backwards into a red, shrieking miasma of disintegrated rock.

Daz was out of the Whistler first. The sonar had been dead on target. In front of them lay the crumpled remains of the two troop transports, buried under tons of rubble. A third transport lay on its side, twisted and broken on the top of the pile.

A photon bolt sizzled over his head.

"Get down!" shouted Eratz, pushing them behind a boulder. He slapped an energy cell into the photon rifle as another bolt pounded the rock. The cell was meant for a hand-held drilling tool, and fitted awkwardly into the slot, but the charge light went green nonetheless.

Daz watched in amazement as his friend bravely spun out from behind their cover and squeezed the trigger. A weak blue beam emanated from the rifle, but it did the job. A cry of pain sounded near one of the destroyed transports.

"When did you learn to shoot like that?" asked Daz, taking the spent rifle from his friend's shaking hands.

"Just now," he beamed.

Morning sunlight streamed through of the hole the Whistler had blown in the ceiling of the tunnel. Climbing over the wrecked transports, Daz made his way to the one on top. The rear doors were smashed open, and something large was jammed in the opening. He pulled away the tarp covering it.

"Eratz, Dr. Havarti...you need to see this!"

"Well, this explains where your artifact came from," said the doctor, pointing out the place where one of five identical wheels was missing.

"Yeah, but what is it?" asked Eratz.

"It looks like an information-gathering rover vehicle of some sort," said the doctor. "This is an amazing discovery."

"It's alien, isn't it?" asked Daz.
"What do you think?" smiled Havarti.

"I knew it. Planetary Security is repressing information about aliens,"

said Daz. "I wonder what else they know."

Eratz smiled at his friend. "I'm sure you're going to make us find out."

"I think the first thing we need to do is bring this to Taal City, although I'm not sure we can trust the city council. They might be involved in the cover-up."

"I have some friends in the scientific community. If we got them to confirm its alien origins, we would have all the proof we need," said the doctor.

"Daz, maybe there's a good reason they don't want us to know about this. How do we know we're doing the right thing?" asked Eratz.

"That doesn't matter. What matters is that they are operating outside the law. No one should be allowed to violate our rights like that."

"He's right," agreed Havarti. "Also, the device looks harmless enough. It looks like it's for research, it's probably not a weapon."

Daz nodded. "Let's see where we are. I want to know where he found it."

Beyond Repair

Earth | *Cardiff, Wales*
Cadogan Aerospace Mission Control Center

The images from the Outlander-I were disastrously ruined. The control room was in an uproar. Cadogan's last minute attempt to shake free the broken glass had failed. He felt both horrified and relieved.

"Roberts, did the probe receive the new landing trajectory?"

"Yes, Captain, er...sir. The high-speed re-entry was a bumpy ride, but I don't think that caused this. The stabilizers in the camera compartment would have easily absorbed the shock."

That's probably what happened then—it's too well designed. He cursed under his breath.

"But we're on the surface, correct?"

"Far as I can tell. The maneuvering thrusters fired as expected, and performed perfectly."

Cadogan knew the descent and landing would have been hard. If that didn't free the glass, nothing would. His wife moved closer to him.

"Isn't there anything you can do?" she asked.

"No. We're done here," he said, brushing aside a stray lock of her hair. "At least you're safe."

Cadogan had no cards left to play. There was nothing else. It was over, and he had lost. Cadogan Aerospace would be ridiculed into bankruptcy and the privatization of space would be set back another ten years.

The conference room in the adjoining building was packed with reporters. Cadogan couldn't hide from them in the control room much longer. The conference room's video feed had only about a two-minute processing delay, so they would be clamoring for him soon.

"I suppose I should explain things to the press."

"What are you going to tell them?" asked Martha.

"What I'm supposed to. That the lander had a major malfunction in its optics. What else is there?"

"They're going to ask why."

"I'll spout the usual boilerplate scientists use when they don't have the slightest idea of what to say. I'm simply say it's too soon to tell, but an investigation is under way."

"That's not going to buy you much time."

"I know, but unless something else comes up, the lander is on its own."

The Outlander-I rested heavily on the sand, crackling and popping as it cooled. The ceramic heat shield was blackened and cracked, but the lander had arrived fully intact. Three legs now supported its large, gumdrop-shaped body.

With a hiss, its three main thrusters purged themselves of residual water vapor. The thrusters employed billions of tiny nano-motors which converted gold and hydrazine into pressurized jets of water. When combined, the jets provided an efficient, powerful way to maneuver the wardrobe-sized lander.

Beneath the fuselage, a camera worked desperately to adjust its lens, backing it in and out, but never quite achieving focus. The sound of its servo whirred loudly over the broken alien landscape. The noise hadn't gone unnoticed.

"What do you suppose the private investigator was trying to tell you?" asked Martha.

"He said we're in danger. But bloody hell, I already knew that. What else could they possibly want from us?"

"Maybe they found out about your attempt to clear the lens."

"So soon? I doubt it. We would have gotten another call by now. That smug bastard would be rubbing my face in it by now."

Someone coughed near Cadogan's shoulder. Turning from his wife, he found Roberts waiting for him, looking grave.

"They're asking for us in the press room, Captain."

Visitor

Mars | *Taal Lesser Dessert, Asper Crater*

Daz helped Eratz and Dr. Havarti over the ruined transports and out of the sinkhole. The cavity the Whistler made was larger than he expected. Rivulets of sand slowed their bid for the surface.

Daz scanned the horizon. The crater's ridge towered above them, casting a long shadow in the cold morning light. He thought he heard distant thunder—a rare sound on his planet. He recognized the outcropping where he had found the wheel. The alien rover they discovered in the Commander's wrecked transport must have been found somewhere nearby.

He thought he heard the rumble of distant thunder, and felt something wet on his cheek. *That's not possible, it never rained anymore.* He looked up.

"Run!"

A huge machine, bellowing steam and hot jets of water fell out of the sky. The trio ran in opposite directions as the craft slowed its descent. Three legs extended from beneath it, each ending in a round pad. With a muddy thump, it settled into the hot, saturated sand.

"What in the name of Taal is it?" asked Eratz, after it was cool enough to approach.

"I don't know, but it's making a weird noise," said Daz.

Dr. Havarti looked underneath the strange machine and found where the sound was coming from. He reached his hand into a recess.

"Doc, I don't think you should—"

A shower of glass shards fell out and the whirring stopped. The doctor jerked his hand away and sucked at his finger.

"Ouch."

"What did you do?" Daz exclaimed. "That thing is from another world. We probably shouldn't mess with it!"

"No, you probably shouldn't," said a hoarse voice behind them. "Now, back away from the craft."

The Commander's left arm hung limply at his side, but his right held a photon rifle. He was covered in dust and his breathing came in painful gasps. He looked like someone back from the dead—Daz thought he might be.

"The relief transport will be here soon." He pointed the rifle at Havarti. "Until then, you'll stay here with me. You two will go back down and retrieve the alien rover. Don't try anything foolish or the doctor gets pulsed."

The Commander watched them leave, then turned his eye to the new machine squatting on the sand like a gigantic three-legged *sand cow*. He allowed himself a painful smile. *Three escaped prisoners, and TWO alien artifacts. The old man will be pleased indeed.*

"I thought you shot him?" asked Daz, sliding down next to his friend.

"I must have just winged him. I'm sorry, I should have checked."

Daz sighed. "It was my stupid idea to come here in the first place. This is all my fault. Now we're all going to die."

He kicked angrily at the jammed door of the transport. It fell off its hinges and clanged to the ground. The alien rover inside leaned over precariously. Eratz jumped forward, barely catching it before it fell out of the vehicle.

"Easy buddy. Let's not give solider boy up there a reason to get trigger happy, okay?"

"It's already broken, how much more damage could we do to it?" said

Daz, eyeing the battered, weathered machine. "By the way, how are we going to lift this thing?"

"It's not that heavy. The two of us should be able to shove it out of here."

The two boys pulled the alien rover out of the transport.

Daz wondered where it came from, and who made it. Something this large should weigh more than it did. The people that made this thing must be very advanced.

"The doc thinks it's alien, and I agree with him," said Eratz, apparently thinking along the same lines.

"But why? What was it looking for?"

"I dunno, but it's sure got a lot of instruments attached to it." Eratz slipped, and an antenna broke free as he tried to regain his hold. It tumbled to the bottom of the debris pile. "Oops! I hope they don't miss that." Daz sighed. "C'mon, let's get it out of here."

"They've gotten what they wanted, so why are we still alive?" asked Daz, sitting next to his friends.

"I was thinking much the same thing," said Dr. Havarti. "Funny how they put us back in the same cell."

"Well, I don't think your little trick with the lighting panel will work twice," said Eratz. "Got any other ideas?"

Before he could answer, the door opened and an armed guard entered the room. Two more were waiting in the hallway outside.

"The Inquisitor wishes to speak with you."

The three companions stood up, but the guard waved two of them down.

"No, just you." He took Daz by the arm and escorted him out of the room.

A Helping Hand

***Earth** | Cardiff, Wales*
Cadogan Aerospace Mission Control Center

The image drew itself line by horizontal line on the view screen. A *clear* image. An image of the ruddy Martian surface. Halfway through the process, the image revealed something else—*a red, four-fingered hand.*

The control room went deathly silent, then everyone started speaking at once. *Aliens?* Was Mars inhabited? Was this some sort of joke?

"A technician took Cadogan by the hand and shook it. Congratulations, sir! You've done it." He handed him a print-out of the final image.

Cadogan stared at it. He didn't know what to say. Too many emotions were competing for his attention.

"Sir, can I speak to you privately?" asked Roberts.

"Um...sure," he said, as if in a dream.

Cadogan and his wife met the chief science officer in his office down the hall from the control room.

"Roberts, I need to get back in there. Make this quick."

"Yes, Captain. What I wanted to say was—"

An explosion rocked the building. The door to the office splintered into the room, knocking them over the desk. Cadogan got Martha and Roberts to their feet, and ran into the smoking hall. A fire was raging inside the control room. No survivors.

He heard running footsteps. *Had someone gotten out*? Turning around, he saw Roberts with four men in HAZMAT gear. *Firemen? Already?*

One of the men grabbed Cadogan sharply, pinning his arm behind his back. He saw his wife restrained as well. These weren't firemen.

"Roberts! Do something," he shouted.

"I am doing something, Captain," said the chief science officer. "These people work for me. You and your wife are now prisoners of the *Protectorate*. "

"What are you talking about?"

"The explosion was regrettable, but the world is not ready to know about life on Mars. Naughty, naughty—Captain."

"You, Roberts? You're behind all this?" Cadogan kicked at the man holding him against the wall, but he couldn't break free. He wasn't going anywhere.

The chief science officer explained. "The Protectorate works to maintain Earth's best interests. Sometimes that means protecting her people from themselves."

"But all those technicians in the control room! You've killed them!" said Martha.

"Actually, your husband's actions sealed their fates. The evidence had to be destroyed."

"What evidence? What are you talking about?" asked Cadogan.

"Proof that intelligent life exists on Mars, of course," said the American.

"There's no life there. Mars is a frigid, barren wasteland," said Cadogan, tired of talking with this lunatic. "We've sent countless space probes which have proved that."

"Cadogan, I know how many tin cans we've lobbed at Mars since the sixties. But you don't know everything about the program. For example, in 1971,

Russia sent two identical probes to Mars, each with its own lander and orbiter. One lander crashed on the surface, but the other arrived in an area called the Terra Sirenum."

"Yes, I know. It didn't last long. There was a dust storm at the time."

"Correct. But that was only a cover story. Do you remember the partial photo it took before the transmission ended?"

Cadogan nodded. He knew the distorted image well. It was the first image take from the surface of an alien world. It reminded him of the Outlander-I's first attempt—an image hopelessly corrupted.

"Here's the one the public didn't get to see." Roberts showed him a picture on his phone. It showed a barren desert landscape, with one important exception. On the distant horizon, tall spires formed the skyline of a sprawling city.

"Everything you know about Mars is a lie. Ever since that first Russian probe landed on Mars fifty years ago, we've known it's a very active, very much *alive* planet. Shiaparelli and Lowell were right—there are canals on Mars, many of them. They connect the *cities.*"

"That can't be," said Cadogan. How could everything he knew about Mars be wrong?

"Even if it were true, why would you hide it?" asked Martha.

"Our world was a very different place back then. We were dealing with Vietnam, the Cuban Missile Crisis and the constant threat of nuclear Armageddon. The last thing we needed was to throw life on another planet into the mix.

"Maybe it's exactly what we needed. Something the world could get behind," said Martha.

"That's a nice sentiment, but naïve. We don't know the extent of their technology, but the Martians are quite capable of disabling our landers and possibly our orbiters. We suspect they may have ballistic missiles. Until we learn what kind of threat they pose to Earth, we can't let the public know about them."

The Chair

Mars | *Taal Lesser Dessert, Asper Crater*

The Commander shoved Daz to his knees in the middle of a large hanger. All around him were artifacts similar to the ones they brought with them from the crater. Other unfathomable apparatus, decidedly not alien, but strange nonetheless, filled the room. The rover and the three-legged flying lander occupied a space near what Daz could only vaguely call a *chair.*

Seated in it was Special Inquisitor Kul. He wore a heavy leather helmet, riveted with metal fittings, which connected him to a myriad of tubes and cables. They ran to different parts of a very disturbing machine. It thrummed and throbbed in his head. It hurt to look at, as if parts of it were in another dimension.

"I had you brought here because I want you to witness something." Kul's eyes were glowing with a fierce white light. More startling was that when he spoke, his lips weren't moving.

Daz tried to ask how this was possible, but his words were lost in an orange and red haze, filling his head.

"This device was discovered by us many years ago. It was used by the ancients to control the minds of not just our people, but those of the *humans* as well. It's a very useful machine."

The ancients? The humans? What was Kul talking about? Daz's head reeled.

"Planetary Security discovered an ancient underground city many years ago. It's long extinct inhabitants left behind amazing machines we are just now beginning to understand. Even so, our technology is still far short of that of the humans."

"What are humans?" Daz asked feebly, trying to maintain his grip on reality.

"They are the ones responsible for all of this." He waved to the alien artifacts. "They've been watching us with their space probes, and with the help of this apparatus, we've been watching them."

Kul turned a large knob on the chair's console and his eyes glowed brighter. "Until now, our governments had a mutual understanding. That situation has changed."

An image of a room with a large view screen floated into Daz's head. People in white lab coats leaned over various instrument panels. To his surprise, their skin was lightly colored, and they had no horns. Nor, to his horror, did they have tails!

"This image is coming from the third planet from the Sun. The humans call it *Earth*."

Daz was stunned. Everyone suspected the third planet could support life, but no one knew for sure. Rocketry was a new technology and still in its infancy. They had rockets and missiles, but breaching the incredible distance between worlds was out of the question.

"We've known for some time that life existed there. The ancients knew of their potential thousands of years ago. They used machines like this one to instill fear and hatred into their society. To a human, the image of a Martian is the embodiment of evil."

"What happened to the ancients?"

"Unfortunately, the humans weren't the only ones that practiced war. Our ancestors self-destructed, taking most of our world with them in total, nuclear annihilation. The loss of technology and the accelerated evaporation of our oceans is their legacy to us."

"Why still hide all of this? We should be helping each other!"

Kul cackled repulsively. "I am going to help them. I'm going to help them kill a very troublesome Earth man, and then I'm going to kill you."

Daz saw many humans in the image of the control room in his head. None of them looked very violent, much less deserving of death. He wondered which one of them Kul had picked to die and why.

In his heightened state, Kul could easily read his mind. "I'm after the one whose eyes we are looking through now. The one that built and sent *that* spying device." The Inquisitor pointed to the large flying lander.

Daz watched the man get handed a photograph. To Daz's astonishment, it showed a red, four-fingered hand. It must have been taken of Havarti when he was inspecting the craft.

"As you can see, he has an image of us. He never should have gotten this far. I've tried to stop him for some time, as has his own government, but his will is strong," said the Inquisitor. "He's been led to believe Mars is a dead world, but now he has proof otherwise."

The scene in Daz's head changed. They were no longer in the control room. Somewhere an explosion had occurred and smoke filled the air. People were yelling at each other in a hallway.

Kul laughed his horrible laugh. "You see. The governments on Earth want him dead as well. He's going to regret the day he had the idea to send that space probe to our planet."

He increased the power. "I rarely use this to kill, it's rather an unsettling process."

"No!" Daz shouted. He lunged for Kul, but the Commander behind him was quicker. The two adversaries rolled on the floor. The Commander's burned arm was useless in the fight, but he managed to restrain the youth.

"How can killing an innocent life on another world possible help us?" asked Daz.

"Its because of people like him that these probes are developed and built. They must be stopped."

"What are you so afraid of?"

"They are much more advanced than we are. Our only protection is that they not discover this with any certainty. Our understanding of the ancient technology is growing. In time, we will exceed the abilities of the humans. Until then, we need to buy as much time as possible."

"So that we can invade them instead?" asked Daz sarcastically.

"If that suits the needs of our people, then yes. Our world is dying. The Earth has a wealth of resources. Over three quarters of its surface is covered in water. We will take what we need to survive."

Dispelling Demons

Earth *| Cardiff, Wales*
Cadogan Aerospace Mission Control Center

Cadogan fell to his knees and gripped his head. "Aaaugghh!"

To say the demon was back was an understatement. It exploded into his head, filling his mind with a gaping maw of sharp teeth, tearing at his soul.

His wife fell to his side and glared at Roberts. "What's happening to him? What have you done?"

"It's not us. It's the Martians. I've seen them do this before. They like their privacy as well. I don't think they like your husband very much."

"Do something!" she shouted.

He took out a small device out of his pocket. "I don't know why I'm doing this. I should just let them have him."

He placed it on Cadogan's forehead and it flashed briefly. The hellish image in his head slowly began to shrink and fade. The devil's face turned to one of surprise, then anger, then agony as it was sent screaming back into the void.

Cadogan looked up at him, panting, "What...what happened?"

"This is a beta-wave inhibitor. It causes a feedback resonance back to the source. The Martians rarely kill people, so we've never had a chance to test it until now. Looks like it worked."

"That demon was a Martian?" asked Cadogan, perplexed.

"Yep. Horrid looking little buggers aren't they? They aren't going to like my using it, but screw them." He helped Cadogan to his feet. "Look Trevor, I like you, and you've seen first-hand what they are capable of. I want you to help us."

"How is it that no one else knows about these creatures?" asked Martha.

"Only the RKA, NASA, and recently, the ESA, have sent probes to Mars. The *Protectorate* maintains tight censorship on all of these agencies, so we completely control what we want the public knows about Mars. Who's to prove us otherwise? Terrestrial telescopes can't resolve nearly enough detail. Why do you think we discourage private enterprise for deep space? We won't be able to keep a lid on this if everyone keeps going out there."

Cadogan considered all the resistance he had met during the project's development. It all made sense now, and it infuriated him. Private enterprise needed to move into deep space. Finding and dealing with dangerous situations was part of the game. If the *Protectorate* could hide something of this magnitude, that showed a power no one should wield. They had to be stopped.

Cadogan froze. Something was in his mind again, but it was different this time, less invasive. It was asking for permission to speak.

Martha noticed her husband's eyes glaze over. He looked a thousand miles away. Roberts rambling on about the *Protectorate*, and didn't seem to notice. She was about to say something, when her husband stopped her.

Giving Martha a quick wink, he turned to Roberts. "What if I agree to suppress information from the Outlander-I? Will you let us go?"

Roberts beamed. "Certainly, captain. Also, don't worry about what you'll do after Cadogan Aerospace folds up. I'm sure I can find a place for you in the organization. Now, let's go meet the press."

"The explosion is sure to have everyone asking questions," said Roberts, but don't worry, we'll handle the fire chief. "Tell them a faulty gas main is suspected. Don't mention that last image."

"Can I at least apologize for how you murdered the technicians?" asked Cadogan through gritted teeth. He couldn't believe the way Roberts so casually dismissed their deaths.

The American scowled at him. "Look Trevor, I'd like to trust you. But if you say anything to give me reason to kill your wife, I won't hesitate to do so. Just be a good little puppet and do what I say."

"If I'm going to be part of this, you need to tell me what you've been hiding about Mars."

"I don't see the harm." said the chief science officer as they walked. "It's still pretty much a barren wasteland, although it's not as cold as you've been told, and the air is quite breathable."

"How spread out are the people? Do they have many cities?"

"Our orbital probes have sent back dozens of pictures of both modern and ancient civilizations. The Cydonia region looked like it once could have been a bustling metropolis, four times larger than New York city."

Cadogan remembered a controversial image he had seen of the area. Conspiracy theorists called it the *Face on Mars*. Apparently, with all the power the Protectorate wielded, some images got past their censors. He wondered if they had murdered anyone for releasing it.

"You said the demon in my head was a Martian. Why do they look that way?" asked Cadogan.

"We're not sure about that." Roberts smiled wryly. "It might just be a strange coincidence, but they certainly do look like red devils, don't they?"

"If they have the ability to enter our minds, why haven't they done so on a larger scale?" asked Martha.

"We have an understanding with the Martians. Neither of our governments wants the public to know about each other. We don't put our landers in major cities, and they don't make themselves known to our people. Over the past fifty years we've been very cautious with each other."

"When do you expect that to change?" she asked.

"The moment we know they aren't a threat. Your leap-frogging lander will be very helpful in that regard."

Electric Chair

Mars | *Taal Lesser Dessert*

Daz felt the human's agony as the Inquisitor overloaded his victim's brain with image after horrible image. Daz watched the event from a distance, but it was intense enough to feel nonetheless. This human was going to die, and there was nothing he could do about it. The Commander tightened his grip, suspecting he might try something.

Without warning, the shared image in his head fell away into a horrible nothingness, dropping behind the solid curtain of reality. The one called Roberts had done something to stop the murdering Kul. As the hanger solidified and reasserted itself, he heard a scream of agony from the chair.

The Special Inquisitor's face contorted with terror and pain. His eyes, no longer glowing, were now two charred, blackened, and smoking sockets. He tore at the helmet, trying to remove it, but he got himself tangled in the wiring. Sparks flew as severed high voltage cables danced over the metal grating beneath the chair. The chair caught fire, engulfing it's occupant.

The Commander let go of Daz, pulled off his jacket and ran to the machine. Kicking the power cables out of the way with his thick boots, he used the jacket to smother the flames. His efforts were in vain, the Inquisitor wasn't moving. He pulled the man out and laid him on the floor.

"Is he dead?" asked Daz.

The Commander said nothing. He did nothing. Oblivious to anything else, he sat crouched over the burned corpse, completely motionless.

Daz quietly picked up a large wrench from one of the workbenches and crept behind the distracted

Commander. He raised the wrench, but something caught him off guard. The Commander's shoulders were shuddering. *Was he crying?*

The Commander leaned his head back and bellowed a deep laugh, taking Daz completely by surprise. Daz fumbled the wrench and it clattered noisily to the floor. Noticing the improvised weapon, the Commander's face changed to one of anger, but only for a moment, then he laughed even louder.

The element of surprise lost, Daz made a run for the hanger door to get away from this maniac. Somehow, he'd find his friends, and get out of this insane asylum.

The Commander held out an outstretched arm and tried to speak between guffaws, "Wait...wait!"

Halfway to the door, Daz heard something that made his stop in his tracks.

"I need you and your friends to fix this machine. I want to help the humans!"

The Commander was finally free to act. His family was now safe, no longer threatened by the mad dictator who had controlled Planetary Security for so long. He could now right the horrible wrongs Kul forced him to commit.

He released Daz's friends and had them brought to the hanger. Daz explained everything that had happened and what they needed to do.

"It's not significantly damaged. I can fix it easily." said Dr. Havarti, reconnecting a few wires.

"Daz, you sure about this? You're sure about *him?*" asked Eratz, indicating the Commander.

Daz smiled at his concerned friend. "Don't get your nubs in a bind, roomie. I'll be fine."

Dr. Havarti completed the last circuit. "This is amazing technology. I've never seen anything like it before. He closed a panel and wiped his hands."

"You're not exactly building my confidence doc," said Daz. He was having second thoughts about the plan he and the Commander had come up with.

"Oh don't worry, it was just a few disconnected cables and the fire was just superficial. This thing looks nearly indestructible."

"Yeah, but you can't say the same thing about his brain," said Eratz, putting the helmet on his friend's head.

"Okay, here we go," said Daz, as the orange and red haze filled his mind.

The human was understandably wary, but the chair had a way of communicating emotion as well as imagery at lightning speed. Daz established a rapport with the man, and each quickly learned what had transpired to the other.

In only a few seconds, they had formed a plan.

The Commander knew he would need to seize control of Planetary Security soon. Not many were loyal to Kul, so the coup would be over quickly—that part was going to be easy.

More difficult would be a full disclosure on the human probes and the ancient technologies. The truth would be shocking at first, but soon, the idea of sharing the solar system with another race would become accepted fact. The two races would learn a lot from each other.

Everything rested on the boy in the chair. He hoped Havarti's repairs would hold. The chair throbbed louder in everyone's heads, but in the boy's hands the experience was far less menacing.

The ancient technologies needed more research. When this was over, he would open the hanger to the public. These miracles of technology had stagnated too long under Kul's greedy control.

The Commander looked at the charred remains of the Inquisitor and smiled. The old regime of fear, greed and violence was finally coming to an end.

Dealing With The Devil

Earth | *Cardiff, Wales*
Cadogan Aerospace Mission Control Center

Cadogan and Roberts walked into the conference room.

"Don't forget about my insurance policy. One word from me and Martha dies," the chief science officer warned. Cadogan noticed for the first time a tiny lapel mic on Robert's collar.

What a fool he'd been to not realize Roberts' treachery earlier. It had cost the lives of five technicians. Good men and women. What would he tell their families? Cadogan took the podium as the bulbs from a hundred cameras flashed in the audience.

"Ladies and gentleman, I am here to announce a tragedy. As you know, there was an explosion in the control room. Besides myself, my wife and my chief science officer, no one else survived. Five exceptional men and women were lost today." He listed the names of those that had perished in the blaze as the questions were hurled at him.

"Was it a bomb?"

"Do you suspect terrorism?"

"What caused it?"

Cadogan waited for the noise to subside, then turned to the mic. Before speaking, he took a quick look at the clock on the back wall. *Any minute now.*

"We don't know all the details yet, but the fire chief tells me it was likely a faulty gas main in the maintenance tunnel below. A full investigation of the accident is underway."

"An accident?" asked a reporter from *MSN.* "The timing here seems a little too coincidental to be an accident. What are you trying to hide, Cadogan?"

"I don't know what you are implying, sir, but nothing is worth killing good men and women over."

"Not even this?" The American showed him a copy of the first ruined image from the Outlander-I.

The engineer stared at the photo. The live feed from the control room must have processed and sent it shortly before the explosion. Roberts stifled a grin. Cadogan was being hung out to dry. The clock ticked out another few seconds. *It'll all be over soon.*

"We experienced a malfunction in the camera's optics. I...I can explain—" stammered Cadogan. *Where was she? She should be here by now.* He'd have to take a leap of faith. He straightened up and reached inside his jacket pocket. "That image isn't very clear. Let me give you another."

Unfolding the printout the technician had given him from his inside pocket, he handed the reporter the photo of a four-fingered hand superimposed over the thick dusty surface of Mars.

Roberts cursed and turned his head to speak into his mic. Instead of issuing a command, he screamed in pain and clawed at the sides of his head. He fell to his knees, pleading for it to stop. His eyes rolled back and he fell over, unconscious.

Three similar cries of dismay echoed outside the conference room. A burly man in a HAZMAT suit staggered inside and collapsed against a wall, his eyes wild with fright. A trickle of blood dripped from his right ear. He shuddered one last convulsion then slid to the floor, a lifeless mountain of flesh. Through the open door, Cadogan could see the big man's two motionless companions. They had shared his fate, their faces a rictus of abject terror.

One of the men still held limply to the arm of someone trying to pull free.

"Martha!" shouted Cadogan, making a dash for his wife.

"All of a sudden they were in a trance. They stopped playing cards, opened the door and let me go," said Martha. "One of them tried wrestling with whatever was controlling him. He was able to block my exit until whatever he was fighting caused him scream. It was horrible."

Cadogan hugged his wife, "Don't worry. Everything is going to be fine."

The reporters surrounding the couple weren't sure what to think. Too many things had happened too fast. No one seemed able to form any of the thousands of questions that needed answering.

The American reporter stepped in front of Cadogan, as if the engineer was going to make a run for it in the confusion.

"I don't know what all this is about, but are you seriously asking us to believe this is a picture of a Martian?" He held up the print out for everyone to see.

Cadogan nodded, and the room erupted into further derision.

Martha turned to her husband, "Trevor, what's going on?"

"Something wonderful, dearest. Just wait a moment and you'll see—*everyone will.*"

A stunned silence filled the room and everyone stopped moving. It was as if someone had flipped a switch, freezing time and setting the volume to mute. Even his wife had relaxed into the quiet, still stupor. He smiled, knowing that behind each of those glassy-eyed stares he would find a vivid image of a smiling, devilish-looking creature waving a four-fingered greeting.

Daz was introducing himself. Soon, everyone on Earth would know what Martians looked like.

The End

Cadogan stood on the bridge of the *Arroyo*. The console in front of him displayed twenty other ships in orbit around Mars. So little time had passed, yet things were happening faster than he could keep track of them.

After that crazy Martian showed himself to every woman, man and child five years ago, all of Earth had faced an identity crisis. Human were no longer alone in the solar system—they never had been. Disbelief, shock and fear rang through the planet.

Unfortunately, the resemblance of Martians to devils didn't help things. The religions of the world were irrevocably shaken to their roots. It would be a long time before people would stop associating them with demons. It might not ever happen.

Maybe Roberts had been right—we weren't ready. But how could any race ever be ready for news of such magnitude? With the exposure of the Protectorate, the evidence was overwhelming, but many still believed it to be a hoax of some sort, but they would come around in their own time. More and more did every year, as acceptance slowly took hold.

Standing at the console his new experimental ship, Cadogan made sure everything was ready, before Earth and Mars took a historic first step towards peaceful relations.

"It's beautiful isn't it?" asked Martha.

"Worth every second of the three-month journey," said Cadogan, looking out the wide panoramic window at the large red disk, suspended in a sea of stars.

High above the planet flew a fleet of large spacecraft. The ships were a variety of shapes and designs, using a hybrid of human and Martian technology. The ships were incredibly fast, and efficient. As such, aero braking was no longer a necessity. Behind each ship followed an immense mountain of loosely packed ice.

"Do you think we'll be able to help?" asked Martha.

"Not in the long term, but the ice runs from Ceres will feed their crops and fill their reservoirs until they finish their massive tunnel network."

The console beeped that the fleet was in position over the major cities. Cadogan gave the order for them to deposit their immense cargos into the atmosphere.

* * *

Daz was rather enjoying his job as Tunnel Excavation Supervisor. The Commander had made it clear the boy would never have to work again, but Daz wanted to earn an honest living just like everyone else. And besides, his simple duties as Excavation Supervisor gave him a lot of free time to explore the desert.

He turned over another boulder, and found what he was looking for, an ancient fossil of a creature with *fins*. He stared at it wonderingly; he must be standing in an ancient seabed. He looked around at the dry, arid landscape, trying to imagine what it would have looked like millions of years ago.

A little puff of dust formed at this feet. He looked down and noticed a round patch of dampness near the spot. Another puff, and then another. Soon, round patches of moisture covered the ground. They appeared faster and faster. Little wet craters filling the ancient seabed.

Daz looked up at the expansive blue sky. His face glistened as the droplets fell. He stared in amazement, his open mouth catching more and more of the life-giving water as it turned first into a shower and then a torrent. Whooping loudly, he punched at the heavens and did a little dance. *They were here! They had made it afterall!* He slipped and skidded in the mud, unable to stop laughing. He laughed and laughed. There wasn't a cloud in the sky, but it was *raining.*

www.ingramcontent.com/pod-product-compliance
Lightning Source LLC
Chambersburg PA
CBHW070612120726
47909CB00004B/1193